Taz's Guards

Charon MC
Book 14

KHLOE WREN

Books by Khloe Wren

Charon MC:
Inking Eagle
Fighting Mac
Chasing Taz
Claiming Tiny
Chasing Scout
Tripping Nitro
Scout's Legacy
Mac's Destiny
Losing Bash
Finding Needles
Forging Blade
Taming Keys
Breaking Arrow
Taz's Guards
Shielding Bank

Silky Ink:
Ink & Dust

Iron Hammers MC:
Cujo's Rampage

RBMC: SA:
Spark's rising
Croc's Pledge

Fire and Snow:
Guardian's Heart
Noble Guardian
Guardian's Shadow
Fierce Guardian
Necessary Alpha
Protective Instincts

Other Titles:
Fireworks
Scarred Perfection
Scandals: Zeck
FireStarter
Deception
Kings of Sydney: Daniil
Mine To Bear
The Warrior, The Witch
and The Wombat
Insatiable Ghost Monster

ISBN: 978-1-922942-03-6
Copyright © Khloe Wren 2023

Cover Credits:
Model: Stefen Northfield
Photographer: Golden Czermak of FuriousFotog
Digital Artist: Khloe Wren
Editing Credits:
Editor: Carolyn Depew of Write Right

Acknowledgements

As always, huge thanks to my husband and daughters for their ongoing support and patience.

Thanks to Stacey for all her research help on all things military and Texan. To Vicki and Erin for their cheerleading and check ins.

And a huge thanks to my readers for being patient with me releasing books out of order! Due to Shielding Bank being tied into an event, and me running out of time, Shielding Bank came out a few months before Taz's Guards. I know that frustrated a lot of people, and trust me, it seriously messed with my own OCD issues too. For all our sanities sakes, hopefully I'll not ever need to do it again!

Happy reading
xo
Khloe

Biography

Khloe Wren lives in rural South Australia with her husband, two daughters and an ever changing list of animals!

She started writing in 2013 and has published over 50 books since then in the romantic suspense genre. She writes both paranormal and contemporary stories, including her best selling series Charon MC.

Khloe enjoys writing outside of the box and she loves her heroes strong, and her heroines even stronger.

Charon:

Char·on \ˈsher-ən, ˈker-ən, -än\

In Greek mythology, the Charon is the ferryman who takes the dead across either the river Styx or Acheron, depending on whether the soul's destination is the Elysian Fields or Hades.

Dedication

Erin, thank you for all you do.

Chapter 1

Thursday 28th March 2019
Flick

After a late-night phone call from my old boss, I couldn't sleep. I'd be up pacing, checking on every little noise I heard, if it wouldn't wake Taz and have him asking questions I didn't want to answer just yet. I couldn't live like this. In the morning I'd go to the clubhouse and corner Scout, and let him decide what we should do with this new information the FBI had dumped in my lap.

With a moan, Taz started thrashing beside me, lost in a nightmare. He didn't get them often anymore, but with only ten days till the anniversary of his mother and sister's deaths, it wasn't a surprise he was having one tonight.

Rolling over onto my side, I took in my man for a few moments. The moonlight streaming in through the break in the curtains showed me the deep frown lines that marred his face as he battled his subconscious. The stubble on his jaw roughened his usually clean-shaven jaw, making him sexier in the dim light. Him mumbling

"Gracie" in his sleep snapped me out of my daze.

I mentally slapped myself upside the head. Taz's subconscious was torturing him with memories best left alone and I was lying here, taking in how sexy he looked with some scruff on his jaw.

"Taz! Babe, wake up."

I was nervous to touch him while he was still sleeping. He was stronger than me, and if he lashed out and hurt me, he'd never forgive himself. But when my voice wasn't enough to rouse him, I pressed up against his side. Touching as much of my body against his as I could while I cupped his jaw in my palm and kissed his cheek, I winced a little at the prickle of his scruff against my soft lips.

"Wake up, Taz. Come back to me."

"Flick?"

His voice was groggy with sleep, but his movements were fast. In seconds, he was on his side facing me, his arms banded tight around me, holding me hard enough I had to breathe shallowly while he buried his face into my neck and shuddered.

I ran my palm up and down his spine, trying to soothe him. My poor man, he'd been through so much in his life, from losing his family in a fire at thirteen, to being shipped halfway around the world to live with a cold, unfeeling aunt. Then there was what he'd seen and done while in the Marines. I'd be more shocked if he didn't have the occasional nightmare.

With another moan, he loosened his hold and slipped

one hand up into my hair. The sting of him tugging on a fistful lit a fire straight to my pussy. Before I could say a thing, his mouth was on mine, hungrily kissing me until my mind emptied of all thoughts but those about how well my man could love on me.

Releasing my hair, he rolled me onto my back, and leaving a trail of kisses and nips, he moved down to my breasts. Kneading one in his big, callused hand, he suckled the other nipple into his mouth, alternating between hard, sharp tugs and gentle swirls of his tongue. He'd mastered exactly how to get my motor purring in no time at all.

Reaching up, I ran my fingers through his short hair, scraping my nails against his scalp in the way I knew sent shivers down his spine. With a moan, he switched sides, giving my other breast the same treatment with his mouth. His weight was pinning me against the mattress, but that didn't stop me from trying to wriggle my legs out from under him, so he'd be pressed fully between my thighs.

His chuckle was dark as he shifted down and latched onto the flesh just beneath my nipple before he sucked hard, no doubt leaving a mark.

"Dammit, Taz!"

He lifted his head, a sparkle in his eyes as he raised an eyebrow at me.

"You telling me you don't like what I'm doin', hellcat?"

He looked so much younger in that moment. All the

worries from his nightmare gone, he was grinning and looking like a kid in a candy store.

"Just do it faster, Taz."

He shook his head, "Nah, teasing you is half the fun. Gotta teach you a little patience."

I growled when I finally got one leg out from under him. Wrapping it around his waist, I rolled us, smirking now that I was on top. "Or I'll just take what I want."

He laughed again, and I paused to absorb the sound. Joy mixed with my arousal that I'd managed to chase away his demons so completely. Naturally, Taz took advantage of my moment of distraction and wrapped his big hands around my waist. I gasped and slapped my palms against the wall when he lifted me, not stopping until his head was between my thighs.

"Hmm. Think I'll have me a little midnight snack."

Before I could give him a smartass reply, he'd lowered me down and swiped his tongue up my center. Then all I could do was moan and rock my hips against my husband's incredibly talented mouth.

Taz

Hated that I still had that bloody nightmare, but waking up surrounded by Flick's scent, having her soft naked body up against mine, banished all those demons darn fast. Now I had her sitting on my face as I made a meal out of her pussy. Fucking loved how she tasted. Nothing

I liked better to have down my throat than her cream. Looking up at her as she arched her back, thrusting her pretty tits out as she rode my tongue, had my cock jerking with need. Shifting to suckle her clit, I thrust two fingers up inside her, zeroing in on her g-spot, rubbing it just how she liked. I slid my other hand between her thighs to run my fingertip over her rear entrance. Teasing her until she bit her lip to muffle her cry as she came and gave me the cream I wanted.

I lapped at her as she shuddered above me, gently bringing her down from her high until her palms slipped down the wall. Before she went boneless on me, I pulled her down over me and rolled so I was on top of her. With a sweet smile, she wrapped her arms around my neck. Looking into her hooded eyes, I lowered my mouth to hers, to kiss her long and slow.

Running a palm down her side, I hooked my hand under her knee and brought her leg up over my hip. A shudder ran through me when my rock-hard cock slid over her wet pussy.

Once my cockhead rested at her entrance, I broke the kiss and lifted my face until I could lock gazes with her.

"I love you, Flick. More than I thought was possible."

She blinked away the moisture that glossed over her eyes as she pressed a palm to each of my cheeks and drew me back down. "And I love you just as much, Donovan."

As I once again pressed my lips to hers, I thrust forward, burying my cock balls deep in one slide. I moaned at the feel of her silken heat surrounding me.

Nothing beat being inside my woman.

Pulling out, I angled myself so my piercing would hit her just right, then stroked back in. She cried out, breaking our kiss as she slammed her hands on my shoulders, digging her nails in as she tilted her hips with every one of my strokes, taking me as deep as she could. But I wanted more, needed more. Pulling free from her warmth, I didn't give her time to do more than frown before I had her rolled over, ass in the air and my cock back inside her pussy.

"Fuck, Taz. Don't stop."

With a grin, I wrapped an arm around her torso, wrapping my palm around her tit and tweaking the nipple, not slowing my strokes the whole time. Like this, my piercing slid over her g-spot with every thrust. It was only a few minutes before she tensed up and, burying her face in against the mattress, gave a muffled shout as she came. Her pussy clamping down on my dick was enough to have me seeing fucking stars as I followed her over, filling her up as I dropped forward over her. Holding my weight on my arms, I caged her body beneath mine as we both panted and recovered.

As soon as I could manage, I pressed a kiss to the sweat-slicked skin between her shoulder blades before I eased out of her and padded over to the ensuite bathroom to grab a washcloth. Once I had us both cleaned up and the cloth dealt with, I crawled back into bed and wrapped myself around my woman, a deep sense of peace making me sleepy.

"Rock my world every damn time, Taz."

"Hmm," I nuzzled in under her ear, pressing a kiss to the sensitive skin and causing her to shiver. "You do the same for me, kitty. Every day."

With that, I pulled her in flush against me, her the little spoon to my big, and closed my eyes. Confident we'd managed to chase away the nightmares for the rest of the night, at least.

Chapter 2

Flick

I hated hiding shit from my man, but there were some things he was better off not knowing. Especially considering the nightmare he'd had last night.

At least not yet. Not before I knew for certain.

It had taken some early morning sneaking around, but with some help from Scout, I'd made sure Taz wouldn't be at the clubhouse this morning so I could have this meeting with the Charon MC's president and VP.

I'd barely entered Scout's office when he started talking.

"Hey, Flick. What's up that needs all this cloak and dagger shit?"

I looked from where Scout sat at his desk to behind him, where Mac was leaning against the wall as I firmly shut the door.

"It's about Taz's past and me keeping my word. Our deal was if I ever heard from the FBI, I needed to bring it straight to you, so here I am."

Mac didn't move but Scout leaned forward, his gaze

turning serious.

"Tell me."

"My old boss, Greg Cave, got in touch with me last night." Scout's mouth opened, but I held up my palm, silencing what I knew he'd say. "He's not trying to hire me back or anything like that, he just wanted to give me a heads up about something. He'd gotten word from the Australian Federal Police that they suspected Taz's stepdad, Gordon Milani, is on his way here. He was last spotted at the international airport in Melbourne. By tracking the fake identity he used, they've worked out he went on a little world tour that ended in Mexico."

Scout rubbed his hand through his hair. "Isn't he supposed to be in jail?"

I huffed out a breath in frustration. "He was. But he got out six months ago. Early release for good behavior."

At thirteen years old, Taz had been at school when Gordon had strangled his mother and set the place on fire, leaving three year old Gracie to perish in the blaze. Taz had returned home to find the house alight and had run in to try to save his family. He'd found Gracie and brought her out, but he'd been too late. She'd already inhaled too much smoke and had died. Any man who could do such evil deeds on innocents should spend the rest of his days locked up.

Scout's eyes flared with rage. "Fucking bullshit. Man kills his woman and child, he shouldn't ever get to see the fucking light of day again as a free man."

I folded my arms over my chest. "I couldn't agree

more. But it is what it is."

Scout looked over his shoulder. "Mac? You're being awfully fucking quiet. What do you know about this clusterfuck waiting to happen?"

Like Scout, I turned my focus to Mac, one of Taz's two closest friends. Along with Eagle, Mac had known Taz the longest out of anyone in the club. He, Eagle and Mac had been in the USMC together before they'd come to join the Charons. They were as tight as blood brothers and always had each other's backs. So, as Scout had pointed out, he was being a little too calm, as though he'd known the information already.

Mac's gaze cut to me as he winced, then he looked back to Scout. "Sergeant Major Johnson rang me last night with the same intel. He didn't call Taz directly because he was worried Taz would take off on his own without telling the rest of us or coming up with any sort of plan before he went hunting. I was going to talk to you about it this morning, but when you said Flick wanted to see us both, figured I'd wait till after we heard her out before I told you."

Sergeant Major Johnson had been their C.O. in the Marines and like my old boss, he seemed to keep an ear to the ground when it came to things that would affect his men, both past and present.

The growl in Scout's voice was a clear sign the man was not happy, "Next time you tell me as soon as you get intel. A phone call last night would have been good. Hell, we live on the same damn street. You could've walked over to my place and fucking told me."

Mac stood straighter and gave him a nod. "Yes, Prez."

He shifted his gaze between us as he spoke, "Now, have both of you forgotten all of a sudden that Taz is a trained sniper, for fuck's sake? Tell me why we shouldn't just let the man go hunting?"

I shook my head, but Mac spoke before I could. "Because he'll be emotional about it. He didn't get the moniker of Taz because he's from Australia. He got it because when he loses his temper—like, really loses it— he goes fucking nuts. Like the cartoon Tasmanian Devil that spins real fast and destroys everything in its path. The Marines helped him learn to curb that shit, but it's still in there. Pretty sure knowing Gordon is coming his direction will set him off in a huge way."

"Especially considering the date." Instantly I had both men's full attention. If I didn't know them like I did, I might have been intimidated. "We're ten days out from the anniversary of their deaths."

Scout sighed and crossing his arms over his chest, he leaned back, switching his gaze between us again.

"What else did your former bosses have to say? Anything remotely useful?"

Mac shook his head. "Sergeant Major just told me it looked as though Gordon was coming for Taz and to watch out for him. He knows how the club deals with issues like this, knows he doesn't need to tell us what to do with the fucker when we catch him."

Scout turned to me, and I sighed. "At least one A.F.P.

- Australian Federal Police - officer will be sniffing around. They don't require any interaction with us. They'll just be here, keeping an eye on things."

"Another fucking cop. Just what I need." He jabbed a finger at each of us in turn, "Either of you get any more calls, I want to know about it the moment you hang up, got me?"

Feeling like I was five and in trouble with the school principal, I nodded and was quick to echo Mac's "Yes, Prez."

Scout stood from the desk. "Flick, you get back to wherever it is Taz thinks you should be. Mac and I will go pay Keys a visit and see what we can do about tracking anyone new in town. Either of you have a photo of this Gordon fucker?"

Mac shook his head. "Sorry, Prez. Wouldn't know him if I tripped over the bastard."

I sighed. "I can get one, but it might cost me a favor down the line."

Scout looked me in the eye. "Don't go there yet. Let's see what Keys can dig up first. The club doesn't need a debt to the Feds hanging over us if we can help it."

Taz
With a high-pitched squeal, my girl's spoon went flying. Again.

"Lola Grace, you'd have better luck getting food in

your mouth if you quit throwing the spoon away."

"Mamamama."

I grinned at my cheeky daughter, unable to stay even a little mad at her as I collected the spoon from the floor and handed it back to her. Probably should rinse it off, but it was just gonna end up back on the tiles in a few seconds so why bother? Not like the floor wasn't clean. Well, at least it had been before Lolly started eating.

"Yeah, she's still upstairs so I'm all you got for now. But you'll be all hers soon. Your mum thinks she's going to go off to do whatever secret sh- stuff she's been doing all week. But I got news for her."

This no swearing around the kids thing was damn hard. I was getting better, though. I didn't say the whole word that time. Without losing sight of my eleven-month-old daughter, I made myself a coffee before I returned to help her finish off her breakfast. Damn, but she really could make a mess.

I was wiping down both child and chair when Flick came racing down the stairs looking sexy as fuck. What I'd give to have a couple of hours to take her back to bed…

She walked over and gave our girl a kiss to the top of her head, ignoring the way her little hands rose up, clearly wanting to be picked up by her mum.

"Can you drop Lolly at daycare?"

I shook my head, trying to keep a grin off my face as I intentionally put a dent in her plans. "Sorry, luv. I gotta get into the clubhouse early today. Club business."

Old ladies didn't get told about club business, so the fact I didn't have anything club related to do today didn't matter. She'd never know.

She frowned but scooped Lolly out of her highchair. She bounced against Flick, giggling with joy at getting her way. I couldn't help but grin at them. My family. I loved both of them with the entirety of my heart and soul and the fact Flick was keeping something from me did not sit well at all.

I hoped like fuck she wasn't cheating on me. I didn't think I'd be able to survive a betrayal of that magnitude.

"Okay, I'll drop her off. Do you know how long you'll be? Maybe we could do lunch?"

Finishing my coffee, I rinsed out the mug and left it in the drainer before I moved to wrap my arms around my two girls. After blowing a raspberry against Lolly's neck and letting the sound of her giggles and the sweet scent of her baby shampoo soothe me, I shifted to kiss my woman. Running a hand into her thick black curls, I took a firm grip and devoured her mouth. With how she quickly relaxed into me, I didn't think she'd lost interest in me. She'd definitely liked everything I'd done to her last night. Remembering the way she'd pulled me back from hell after my nightmare the night before that reassured me she was still wholly mine, too.

I was still enjoying the hell out of kissing my woman when Lolly declared time-out with a loud scream. And in case we were deaf, she bounced in Flick's arms to the point she nearly slipped from her grip.

"Whoa, baby girl. Settle down or I'll put you back in your chair."

At Flick's stern words, she pouted, clearly unimpressed with her mother's threat.

"You just want all the love for yourself, don'tchya?" I blew another raspberry in against her neck until she was giggling again.

Flick laughed. "You two are as bad as each other. Go on, go do your thing and let me know if you'll get done in time for lunch at Marie's."

"Sure, kitty." I stole a quick kiss before pulling back to hold her gaze. "You know I love you more than life, right?"

Her eyes glossed with moisture for a moment before she leaned in, cupped my cheek and pressed a kiss to the corner of my mouth. "Right back at you. You and Lolly are my whole world. I'd be lost without you both."

I let the silence hang for a moment, giving her a chance to fill it. When she didn't, I gave both her and Lolly another fast kiss before turning to grab my keys. Now certain that whatever Flick was playing at wasn't about her stepping out on me, it was with a grin I waved goodbye and headed out to my bike. I had a mystery to solve, since my woman wouldn't just tell me what the fuck she was up to.

Chapter 3

Taz

Keys was not only the club secretary, he was also in charge of the Charon's latest business venture, Athena Security. That made him just the man I needed today. Athena was so new the club hadn't found premises for it yet, so for now it was being run out of the clubhouse. I walked into the man's office, shutting the door behind me.

"G'day, Keys."

"Fuck off with that Aussie shit, brother. Whatcha want?"

Snickering, I moved to sit in front of his desk. Resting my elbows on my knees, I got serious and looked him in the eye.

"Flick's up to something and I need to know what it is."

He cocked his eyebrow at me. "You tried asking her?"

I sat back, confident I'd be able to get the club's resident tech head to help me.

"Nah, she's being way too sneaky and cagey for a

direct approach. I need you to work your magic and give me intel on what she's up to. She's dropping Lolly at daycare this morning if you want a starting point."

Keys was a paranoid bastard. He had cameras up all over Bridgewater, so I knew with a few keystrokes, he'd be able to track my woman and hopefully tell me what I needed to know.

But instead of getting straight onto his laptop as I'd expected him to do, he sat back and shook his head. "Told them this shit wouldn't go unnoticed. But did they listen? No."

Frowning, I opened my mouth to ask him what the fuck he was on about when he pulled out his phone and indicated I stay quiet.

"Hey, Prez. What I said was gonna happen, happened. You can come explain to the Aussie what's going on because I am not gonna take the heat for this one."

Anger sparked through me. My club brothers—*my motherfucking president*—knew something about my woman that I didn't?

Keys hung up and started tapping at his laptop. "Wait for Scout before you start, brother. He'll be here in a minute, but to make you feel better, let me find where your old lady is."

Scout must have been in his office up the hall as it was only seconds later when he came strolling through the door.

"Hey, Taz—"

That's all he got out before Keys interrupted and had

my full attention.

"Hold up, Scout. Taz, when was Flick heading in to drop off Lolly?"

I stood and moved around to Keys' side of the desk so I could see the video feeds he was switching between. "She should have left about ten minutes after I did."

Hera Daycare was another business run by the club, so Keys had access to the security cameras both outside and in. He also had access to their electronic attendance lists.

"Her car's not in Hera's parking lot, and Lolly hasn't been checked in. Let me search the roads from your place to there. Scout, you've only got a few minutes to get Taz up to speed. I'm calling in Mac."

I turned on Scout, my earlier anger at the betrayal that my club would keep anything about my family from me returning in full force.

"Mac knows too? What the fuck is going on?"

Scout held my gaze with a hard glint to his eyes that told me I wasn't going to like what he was about to say.

"Looks like your stepdad is out of jail and might be heading this way."

I frowned. "That makes no fucking sense. He went away for fucking murder. Even if he did get out, he wouldn't be allowed to leave Australia."

Scout's expression darkened, like he wasn't any happier about this shit than I was. "From what Keys has dug up, Gordon has an uncle who's involved heavily in the criminal underworld in Melbourne. Guessing the motherfucker had strings pulled. Paperwork falsified. The Australian Federal Police contacted Flick's old boss, who got hold of her to let her know. She came to us."

I didn't know where to start processing what Scout had just told me. When the fuck had Keys investigated my past? Since when did Gordon have any connections? As far as I knew, he'd never left the fucking house after he lost his job, and rarely left even when he had work. Certainly, he never had anyone worth knowing come around to visit his sorry ass. Then there was the fact that apparently my own fucking wife, my old lady, didn't trust me?

I picked up the empty coffee mug off Keys' desk and pegged it at the wall. With a loud crash, it dented the drywall before it fell to the floor in several pieces.

"That, right there, is why we didn't tell you. Last thing we need is for you to lose your shit and go off grid with this. We've been monitoring the cameras searching for him but haven't found any indication he's here yet. Flick was protecting you by coming to us."

With my fists clenched, I glared at Scout, roaring my words, "It's me who's meant to fucking protect her! Not the other way—"

Keys cut me off, "Ah, fuck."

The roughness in his voice had me spinning to see what had happened, knowing it would be bad to have Keys cursing. The bottom fell out of my world as my worst nightmare unfolded on the screen before me.

"Oh, no. Fuck no…"

I fell to my knees as I watched my past catch up with my future. Keys had pulled up the camera feed from the one on the front of my and Flick's house. I got to watch in high-definition color as Flick strapped Lolly into her car seat and moved around the SUV. I could see the panic flare on Flick's face when Gordon, who'd rushed up behind her, shoved a syringe into the side of her neck. She glanced up to the camera for a moment before the bastard hit the plunger and drugged my woman.

My voice was low and gravelly with my fury and pain. "I'm gonna kill that motherfucker. Where are they heading?"

Gordon shoved Flick into the trunk of her car before he'd gotten into the driver's seat and driven off. Lolly had to be scared out of her mind. I hoped like hell she stayed quiet so Gordon didn't hurt her.

Keys was running the tracker on the car as well as pulling up various cameras to follow him as Mac came in. I couldn't look at him. My former Gunnery Sergeant had always been a man I trusted completely to have my back in all things, but he was part of this conspiracy to keep Gordon's presence from me, and now the fucker who'd murdered my mum and sister had my woman and daughter. I wasn't sure how I was going to ever trust any of these men — or Flick — again, but that was a problem for another day. Today, my complete focus was on rescuing my family. I wouldn't fail this time.

The tracker program finally loaded up. "Got him. He's headed out of town. I don't have cameras out there, but as far as I know, the only places around are abandoned. There's no way to get out to a highway, so he ain't making a run for it. He's only got a fifteen-minute head start on us."

My voice was more growl than not, but I didn't give a fuck. "A lot can happen in fifteen fucking minutes. I'm getting my gear. Message me his final location as soon as you have it."

I strode toward the door, barely hearing Scout telling Mac to not let me out of his sight. They could all go fuck themselves. They'd kept this shit from me, so they were at least partly to blame for where we were now. I didn't need any of them to help me snipe that fucker and save my family.

I headed to the hidden back stairs and hurried down to the basement. We had cells down here and an armory. I kept my M40 sniper rifle there, and a few other toys. Those of us with little kids stored most of our firepower here. I didn't want Lolly to ever be close to this stuff, even if it was locked up in a safe.

Solidly in mission mode, I collected everything I might need. Stripping my club colors off, I put on a shoulder harness with my M9 Beretta strapped in before I slipped the leather back on and added a spare clip to my collection. Once I had everything either on me or in a backpack, I grabbed the bag along with my rifle case and returned upstairs. When I got to the top, Eagle was there waiting, and a wave of uncertainty hit me. He'd been my spotter in the USMC. It'd been him, Mac and me for as far back as I could remember, but now Mac had torn that apart. Had Eagle?

"Don't you fucking lie to me. Did you know too?"

Holding my gaze directly, he shook his head. "I had no clue, brother. My instincts have been flaring up for days, but I hadn't been able to figure out why. Not till just now when Scout told me what's going down. I've got the location, and Mac's got a cage out front ready to go. I've got your back, brother."

I nodded at him, glad to have him at my six. "I don't want Mac on this."

Eagle took the bag from my hand and shook his head again. "Don't be a fucking idiot. You're hurt over the shit he and the others pulled. I get that. But don't go making this mess worse by cutting him out now. You know he'll do anything to keep you and your family safe. Let's go take care of business, then you can beat the shit outta him or something, okay?"

I rolled my shoulders and cracked my neck as we headed toward the front door.

"Whatever. You and I will get this done."

I didn't have time to waste on trying to work out what I was going to do about anything other than rescuing Flick and Lolly. The mission would come first. Just like always.

Flick

Oh, someone was gonna pay dearly for this shit.

No one got the jump on me and got away with it. Especially if it put my daughter at risk. I had no clue how long I'd been out, but when my brain came back online, it was to the realization that I wasn't alone. Tensing my muscles, I got ready to open my eyes and fight my way out of wherever the hell I was, so I could go find my daughter.

"Shh, stay quiet. He thinks you're still out cold. I gave you an injection to counteract the sedative he gave you. You'll be a bit groggy for another minute or two, then you should be good as gold. I need to go find where he's stashed your daughter, but I'll be back soon."

My eyes refused to open, but I could make out from the quiet voice that whoever was here with me was female and Australian. Her accent was so similar to Taz's I was sure she wasn't English or New Zealander, but Australian. Was this woman with the AFP? My eyes finally obeyed my command to open but before I could see more than a flash of her braid of pale, naturally red hair, the woman was gone, and I was alone.

Whispering to myself, "Okay, then," I looked around the room. I was clearly in an abandoned house. The lumpy mattress beneath me was on an old metal bed frame, high enough I could easily slip off to stand on the rough timber floor. There was a single window that no longer had any curtains or glass that revealed an endless vista of Texas scrubland, proving we weren't in town but somewhere out in the countryside. Focusing back inside, I caught sight of the remains of a full-length oval mirror on a stand in the corner. The shards of the broken glass littering the floor gave me an idea. If I could find one with a point and small enough to grip in my hand, it might just work as a weapon.

I hadn't gotten a look at the man who'd grabbed me, but with how he'd wrapped his distinctly masculine arm around my front to hold me as he injected me, I guessed he was around my height. I figured it was safe to assume it had been Gordon, but honestly, it didn't really matter. Regardless of who had taken us, I needed to neutralize the bastard and make sure my daughter was okay before getting us both the hell out of Dodge.

Loud footsteps coming closer had me snatching up a shard of the mirror and returning to the mattress. Feigning unconsciousness would hopefully give me an element of surprise I could use to overpower him. From the photos Keys had found of Gordon, I knew if this was him, he was roughly my height, but built more solidly than me and would easily outweigh me. He was also in his fifties, so I hoped he was less agile than me. I was fairly certain I was the better trained out of the two of us. Still, getting out of here wasn't going to be easy.

"Well, at least the boy has good taste."

I barely heard the muttered words as he came closer. Like the woman, he spoke with an Australian accent. Further evidence this was most likely Gordon, the man who'd destroyed Taz's world once already and was apparently going to have a go at doing it a second time. Without my sight, I had no clue what he'd do until I felt him wrap his hand in the front of my shirt. When he tugged, clearly wanting to rip the material, I moved into his grip, bringing up the mirror shard as I did. I opened my eyes to see I'd misjudged my aim and instead of getting his throat, I'd swiped it across his cheek.

"Bloody hell! Fucking crazy sheila…"

Now that I could see him, I was sure it was Gordon. He matched the photos I'd seen of Taz's stepdad. With one hand cupped to the slice I'd given him, he swung his other fist at my face. I knocked his arm aside and rolled away. Since he stood up against the side of the mattress, blocking my ability to get off, I shifted to get my feet under me on the bed. Even with my head still a little fuzzy from the drugs, I managed to rise up into a fighter's stance.

"Can see why my boy took a liking to you. Gotta love one that'll fight back."

Fury had my vision going red for a moment as I curled my lip while I lifted my fists in front of me, ready to attack. "Taz has never been your boy."

He shook his head and lowered his hand from his face, ignoring the blood that still trickled from the wound. "Taz? Such a stupid fucking nickname. Donny was a good Italian name. He could've gone a long way in the organization with a solid name like that." He let out a scoff. "Instead, he joined a fucking motorcycle club and took on the name of a cartoon character."

He threw another punch but anticipated my blocking it and grabbed my wrist when I did, tugging me off balance so I fell forward into him. We both went crashing to the ground, with me on top. Stupid idiot had no idea how to fight. I could guess since he was so big and had a scary family, he'd never actually had to attempt hand to hand with anyone who had some skill.

While he was still stunned from crashing into the floor, I landed a one-two punch combination to either side of his jaw before I rolled off and up onto my feet again. My head was completely clear now and as I moved, I swept up another shard of the mirror. He stayed down for a few moments before, with a groan, he pulled himself up to his feet.

"You really are a crazy bitch, aren't you? I'm gonna have fun taming you."

I raised a brow. "You're welcome to try. But I doubt it's gonna end well for you."

He attempted to say something else, but a sweet voice coming from the doorway stopped him in his tracks.

"Hey, Dad. Long time, no see."

With a gasp, he jerked around until his focus was solely on the newcomer. Without dropping my guard, I shifted my gaze and the blood drained from my face when I saw the woman was holding Lolly. The fact my little girl looked unharmed was of little comfort. The tears tracking down her cheeks broke my heart. She clung to the woman, but her baby blues were locked on me, silently begging me to fix her world. Was this stranger working with Gordon or against him?

His voice was rough, barely more than a whisper, "It can't be…"

The woman cocked her head to the side in a very familiar way that had the hair on the nape of my neck standing up.

"Why's that? Because you killed me? Well, surprise! You failed. Turns out Donovon did get me out of the smoke in time."

Gordon stumbled toward the woman and into the shaft of light coming in through the window. A moment later he dropped to the floor, a neat hole through the side of his head. With how his eyes were wide open and glazed over, I knew there was no need to check for a pulse to confirm the fact he was dead.

Relief rushed through me. Gordon was neutralized and Taz was here. Somehow, my man had worked out we were in trouble and was out there with his sniper rifle.

"Mamamama!"

Lolly's high-pitched voice had me wanting to rush to her, but I still wasn't sure whose side the woman was on. From what she'd just said, this was Grace, Taz's sister, and she hadn't sounded as though she was working with him. Gordon certainly hadn't acted like a man who'd known his daughter had survived. But she had Lolly. I couldn't risk my baby girl on an assumption.

"I'll happily hand her over to you, but maybe you could come here and take her? I don't want her near him, even if he is dead. And I don't think my brother would ever forgive himself if he sniped me before he realized who I was."

I started to move toward her, but she took a step back as her gaze locked onto my hand. "Please put that down. I promise I didn't come here to hurt anyone other than Gordon. I came to help keep my brother and his new family safe from him." She nodded down at the body. "That's all."

I glanced down at the mirror shard I still held. It'd cut my hand with how tightly I'd been gripping it. I tossed it aside and wiped my palm on my pants so I could inspect the wound. Happy it was barely more than a scratch and wouldn't need any medical attention, I moved closer to my girl. As I got in range, Lolly reached out, nearly jumping from the other woman's arms toward me.

Taking my daughter from her, I cuddled her close, relieved to be holding her safe against me, even if she was crying in against my neck. I ran my gaze over the woman. Up close, it was clear she was related to Taz. Same blue eyes, same jaw line. But it was still hard to believe that this woman standing in front of me could be Grace, Taz's long-lost sister he'd thought was dead for the past twenty-two years.

"You've got a hell of a lot of explaining to do, Grace. Gordon wasn't the only one convinced you'd died in that fire when you were little."

She nodded with a wince. "Yeah. Let's go find my brother before he starts getting trigger happy and I'll explain."

I pressed a kiss to Lolly's temple, taking a deep breath in of her sweet baby scent before I followed Grace out of the room and toward the front of the old house.

"Maybe I should go out first."

She'd had a point about how Taz would feel if he shot first before he asked any questions. I hoped he was ready for the shock of his life, because this was going to throw him for six.

Chapter 4

Taz

Not wanting to risk alerting Gordon to our presence, Eagle and I set up a distance from where he had holed up. Not that either of us minded. I'd been one of the USMC's best snipers, and Eagle had been my spotter. While it was a few years since we'd had to work together like this, we fell into our roles smoothly and got down to business.

The crack of my M40 firing split the air around me while I kept my gaze down the scope, watching as my bullet hit Gordon just above his ear and his body dropped like a stone.

Eagle's voice was calm, helping me stay in the zone I needed to be in. "Target is down. Good shot."

I kept my gaze on the scope. "There's someone else in there. I caught a glimpse of her earlier but didn't have a clean line of sight to confirm if she was a friendly or not."

Flick walked in front of the window, into my scope's line of sight and I watched as she held out her arms, reaching for something.

"Let's pack up and get in there. There's no way of

knowing if that other person is a friendly or a target. Not from here."

I nodded and stood, grabbing my rifle and jogging over to the cage. We got things packed away quickly — I'd do a better job later of getting it all stowed properly — then we were making our way to the house.

As I headed from the vehicle toward the building with my Beretta in my palm, the sound of several Harleys filled the air. My club brothers coming to have my back. Would Mac be with them? Would Scout? I wasn't sure how to wrap my mind around them keeping such big secrets about my past from me, but it wasn't something I was gonna sort out at the moment. Now, it was time to make sure my old lady and daughter were safe.

And work out who the fuck else was in that house.

With my weapon raised and ready to fire, I began to climb onto what was left of the front porch. The door swung open and when Flick appeared in the doorway clutching Lolly to her, I shifted my aim to the space beside Flick's head, on the opposite side from Lolly. I didn't want to have to risk a shot so close to either of my girls, but if a threat stood behind them, I could take care of it if necessary.

"She's a friendly, Taz. Put the gun away. I'm not bringing our daughter out while you have a gun aimed in our direction."

I hesitated. Any other day I'd do what she told me, but she'd kept shit from me that had led to this situation in the first place.

"Need to make sure you're both protected. Ain't lowering my weapon."

She squeezed her eyes closed for a moment, tightening her hold on Lolly before she returned her gaze to me.

"At least put the safety back on. Trust me, this is going to come as a shock, and you don't want to do anything crazy before your brain processes things."

What the fuck was she on about? Anger shot through me that she had so little faith in me. "How about you fucking show *me* some damn trust and get your ass over here behind me. I'm done fucking around, Flick. You kept shit from me, shit I should've been told about. Instead of trusting me, you went behind my back, and it nearly cost me both of you, my fucking heart and soul."

Even I could hear the ice in my tone, but I didn't give a fuck. I was on edge and in no mood to negotiate a damn thing.

A pained expression passed over her face before she nodded and took a step toward me. She was tense and looked worried I was gonna shoot first and ask questions later. If she didn't hurry the fuck up, she might have reason to be worried. Because so help me, if whoever else was in that house had a weapon trained on either of my girls, I intended to shoot them the second I saw them.

As Flick came closer, I kept my gun aimed on the doorway, steady and ready to fire as I waited for a muzzle flash or any other sign that a target remained in the house.

"Get behind me."

Thank fuck that for once in her life, she didn't argue before she moved to stand directly behind me.

She pressed her palm against my shoulder, her warmth cracking a little of the ice I'd let settle over me. "I'm sorry I didn't tell you about Gordon. You're right, I should have told you, trusted you. Now it's time for you to make a better choice than I did and trust me. You will never forgive yourself if you fire that weapon right now."

Why the fuck did she think I was going to shoot before I saw the threat? Like I didn't have any control over my fucking trigger finger. It'd been a long damn time since I'd lost my temper and gone crazy. The Marines helped me hone that shit into the ice-cold calm I was currently sporting. Clearly, Flick's brother had told her stories about my younger self and somehow, she thought that shit was still how I rolled. Like we hadn't been together for two fucking years, and she didn't know me any better.

Unable to find words, I grunted in response. Lolly's whimper about shattered my heart. When she wrapped her little hand in the sleeve of my shirt, I wanted nothing more than to turn to her. I was scaring my daughter, but I couldn't leave them open to danger. Couldn't put down my weapon until I saw who'd been in the fucking house with them.

"She saved us, Taz. Her actions saved both our lives. Please lower your weapon so she can come out."

For some reason, Flick was clearly set on saving whoever was in that house from me. Wanting to end this shit so we could all get out of here, I yelled, "Come out with your hands where I can see them!"

My world stopped when a woman stepped into the doorway with her arms out, hands facing me. She had to be a hallucination.

"Uh, hey, Donny. I'm with Flick on this one. I'd really appreciate *not* having a gun pointed my way."

There was no way she could really be here. It couldn't be…

Then Eagle was at my side. "Let me have it, brother."

My whole body felt numb, and I didn't even try to resist Eagle as he slipped the gun from my grip. That woman couldn't be my baby sister all grown up. It simply wasn't possible.

"How? I don't understand."

She reached up and rubbed her palm over the back of her neck. "That's a conversation I'd prefer to have somewhere a little more private than this, if you don't mind."

I knew several of my brothers were behind me since their bikes had cut off before Flick had come out, so I wasn't surprised when Scout came up to stand beside me on the opposite side of Eagle.

"Take your family back to the clubhouse, brother. Some of the others will stay and clean this mess up."

I nodded at his words, but it was another few minutes before I could tear my gaze off Grace long enough to act on it.

Jacie

Donny hadn't taken his gaze off me for more than a few seconds since I'd stepped out of that piece of shit house. While one of his buddies drove the car with us back to their clubhouse, he'd sat in the rear seat next to me, his daughter wrapped in his arms as he watched me. Now we were in what looked like a bar that was apparently part of their clubhouse, and he was still staring at me.

"I'm not going to vanish if you look away, Donny."

He just grunted and kept staring at me. His daughter was now fast asleep, secure in her daddy's arms. Seeing my big brother with that little girl was enough to melt my insides. I didn't have many memories from my early years, before I lost everything, but the ones I did have included how great Donny had been to me.

"It's annoying as hell, aint it?"

I turned to Flick, who was coming down the stairs to the rear of the space. There must be bedrooms up there as Flick was freshly showered and in clean clothes now. "What's annoying?"

She nodded toward Donny. "Him. When he doesn't believe you're real. He did it to me once. About drove me nuts."

I scoffed a laugh. I really liked Donny's woman. I couldn't wait to get to know her better.

"How'd you get him to snap out of it?"

She went over and leaned in to press a kiss first to her daughter's head then her man's cheek. "Well, he was drunk as fuck at the time, so I had to put up with it till he passed out. Thankfully, along with his hangover the next morning came some sense."

Donny flicked his gaze to his woman for a moment, frowning. "Different circumstances, hellcat. You weren't dead." Then he was back looking at me.

I sighed. "Did you ever find out about Gordon's family?"

Donny shook his head. "Never gave a fuck about him or his relatives. Once you and Mum were gone and I got shipped over here, I left the past in the past. Although apparently, the club did some digging into him."

Another man stepped in closer to us, who had "Keys" written on a patch on his chest. "We do a little digging on anyone new to the club. We've learned it pays to know what might come at us before it actually does. So, when Taz first came to us, I went hunting for information on his past. Gordon's uncle is a big deal in Melbourne. Publicly, he owns the casino, but under the radar, he runs anything he can get his hands on. Drugs, guns, girls... he's a real piece of work."

I nodded. "Yeah, Uncle Tony is a force of nature. Cops have been trying to get something to stick for decades but no one's managed to do it yet. He's careful, and he's bought off a few key people."

Donny, who I needed to get used to calling Taz apparently, shook his head. "How does any of that fucking explain you coming back from the dead, Grace? I carried your limp body outta that fucking house!"

His daughter stirred, whimpering at her dad's outburst. Flick reached over and took her from him. The little girl quickly snuggled into her mum and with a thumb in her mouth, was back to sleep in moments. My gaze got caught on her for a few seconds. She was such a sweet little girl. I'd only held her for a few minutes earlier, and she'd been scared and upset then. I really wanted to have more cuddle time with her when she was like she was now, all sleepy and relaxed.

"Need some answers, Grace."

With a sigh, I turned my attention back to my brother.

"I did nearly die. I was in a coma from the smoke inhalation, so it was easy to pull some strings to fake my death. You had relatives here in the States that could take you in. I had no one other than Uncle Tony. I was lucky that the AFP took an interest and decided I'd be safer in Witness Protection. They never explained exactly why, but I suspected they were worried Gordon planned to finish off what he'd started." I shrugged, pushing aside those thoughts. Having a homicidal parent wasn't something that brought on warm and fuzzy feelings, even now that I knew he was dead. "I'm not Grace anymore. My name is Jacie Lewis now."

He rolled his shoulders and cracked his neck. "Fuck. Just... fuck it all. They shouldn't have separated us. Why the fuck wouldn't they have put me in witness protection with you? That's bullshit."

He walked away, hands on his hips, pacing the room. There weren't many others around, but those who were,

were completely focused on us. I hated being the center of attention, although it was pretty much a given that my turning up was going to make a splash.

He came back and stood in front of me. "Did you end up in a nice family? Please tell me you had a good life."

I nodded. "I was put with an older couple up in Canberra. They adopted me and were good to me. My new dad was an officer with the AFP. I followed him into the force. I knew early what I wanted do and worked my ass off to get there."

He folded his arms across his chest. "Was that how you knew Gordon had skipped out?"

I nodded. "Yeah. I'm an Operations Engineer in the Digital Surveillance department. As soon as that bastard got out, I set up alerts on him. If there hadn't been a big incident at the Sydney Airport that needed my complete focus, I would have caught the notification earlier and been able to prevent him from leaving the country. Instead, it took me a little time to track down his location. He didn't fly directly to the US." I didn't want to talk about Gordon anymore. Hell, I'd be happy to never hear his name again, and we all knew that he'd ended up here. "How about you? Did your aunt treat you well?"

He raised an eyebrow. "Well, she fed me regularly, so I guess I can't complain."

Flick scoffed. "If that old bitch was still breathing, I would've gone to teach her a fucking lesson. She was horrible to your brother."

Donny shrugged, looking uncomfortable. "I survived.

It wasn't so bad. I enjoyed working on the ranch."

That confused me. "But you left to join the Marines when you were eighteen?"

He glared at me. "How'd you know that shit?"

I rubbed a hand over the back of my neck and looked at the floor for a moment before returning my gaze to his.

"You're my brother, Donny. I was curious. Can we sit down? Maybe get a drink or something?"

One of the men standing near called over to the bar and a younger guy came over to take our drink orders, but no one paid for anything. Strange, but whatever. I asked for a beer and a bottle of water before sitting down on a nearby couch. Flick sat next to me and as she settled back, I couldn't help but smile at her sweet baby girl.

"What's her name?"

Flick winced a little and didn't look like she wanted to tell me. Surely the child's name wasn't some big secret?

Taz's voice was rough with emotion as he answered me. "Lola Grace. We all call her Lolly."

"Oh." Tears pricked my eyes and I blinked rapidly to clear them. He'd named his daughter after me and our mum. A tribute to his lost family.

Chapter 5

Taz

The way Jacie was battling tears after learning Lolly's full name left me rubbing my chest to ease the ache. She'd grown into a spitting image of our mother. The long, curly pale red hair, the blue eyes, the freckles over her cheeks—everything about her was like having Mum back in the room. It was a lot to process, especially when I wasn't sure how long I'd have her around.

As much as I didn't want to interrupt the moment she was having watching Lolly sleep, I had to know. "What are your plans now that your job is done?"

When she shifted her gaze back to me with a wince, I mentally prepared myself for her to say she needed to head off today.

"Well, since chasing down Gordon wasn't technically my job, I'm sure I'll be in trouble when I do go back. He shouldn't have warranted even being on the AFP's radar, really. At least not before he left the country. Which we wouldn't have known about if I wasn't using police resources without permission to monitor him. Not to mention I need to somehow explain how he's now dead without getting you in trouble."

I stiffened when Mac came over, moving from where he'd been at the bar over to us.

"There is no body, Jacie. Not sure how much you know about MCs, but we take care of our own. That includes cleaning up any messes. The house and body have been dealt with. So, as far as the AFP is concerned, Gordon Milani is missing. You could go home and report that he never turned up and once you explained the situation to your brother, he assured you he could handle him if he does ever show up."

Scout came in through the front door as Mac had been speaking. He headed over to the bar and grabbed a drink before coming to join us just as Mac finished.

"You know, if you wanted to stay here, get to know your brother and his family, you're welcome to. We could actually use someone with your skills."

She frowned at the club president. "While I might have bent some rules a little in this situation, I have no intention of switching sides and making a habit of it."

I bit my cheek to not grin at her sass.

Scout smiled and took a swig of his drink before he responded, "The Charon MC is above board, mostly. Our newest business is called Athena Security and we could genuinely use your skills. If you were interested, I'm sure we could sort out a work visa to get you here all legally and shit."

Jacie—damn, but it was taking time to wrap my head

around not calling her Gracie—sat motionless, staring blankly at Scout like he'd made his offer in French or something.

Flick chuckled and bumped her shoulder into Jacie's. "Not sure where you've been staying, but if you do decide to move here, you could live with us until you find your own place. We have plenty of room, and having another adult around to chase Lolly is always a plus."

Flick looked to me with a raised eyebrow, and I took the hint.

"Yeah, we'd love you to come stay with us. For however long you want. And Scout's not blowing smoke up your arse, that job offer is genuine too."

Realizing I was barely making sense, I stopped talking and finished off my whiskey while I waited for Jacie to say something.

"Well, I think deciding to move from Australia to the US shouldn't be a knee-jerk decision made in the heat of a moment. But I'm sure I can at least call in some leave to spend a couple weeks here, considering the circumstances. And I'm staying at the motel in town, which is nothing special, so I won't complain about leaving it to stay with my big bro."

I frowned. "What about your job? If you're gonna get in trouble, won't they want to haul your arse over the coals sooner rather than later?"

A blush pinkened her cheeks. "Since my dad is my boss, I'm sure I can convince him to hold off on the grilling I'm due until I go home. He knows our history."

I shook my head. "Un-fucking-believable. I need another drink."

She had me thinking she might be going to Federal fucking prison or some shit when really, she was just going to get a lecture from her adopted dad. To the sound of Flick chuckling, I walked over to get a refill. While I waited for the prospect to pour it, Mac came over and leaned against the bar beside me.

"The only reason we didn't tell you was because we didn't have confirmation he was actually in town."

I turned to glare at one of my oldest friends. "Cut the fucking bullshit, Mac. You didn't tell me because you all thought I was going to go off grid to go on a rampage till I found the bastard. Tell me, mate, when was the last time I lost my cool?"

He raised an eyebrow. "You threw that mug in Keys' office earlier."

I rolled my eyes. "You know what I mean. The last time I went all Tasmanian devil… when was it?"

With hands on his hips, he looked up to the ceiling as he thought.

"Been a long damn time, huh?" I turned to fully face him. "I don't lose my cool anymore. You, of all fucking people, know that. I'm ice-cold calm when I get mad, and when I hunt, I have all emotion turned off."

Mac shook his head. "In any other circumstances, I'd agree with you. But this was your stepfather, the man who'd killed your family once and was potentially coming for your current one. But it wasn't even that.

Okay, yeah, I was worried you'd lose that well-trained, cool front you have now, but more than that, I didn't want you to have to face that asshole again. I wanted to be able to step in and deal with it so you wouldn't have to. Hell, brother, it's only been what? Six months since you worked over Volt. You're always the one who does the rough interrogations, and that shit has to be building up in your head. I wanted to be able to take this one off your plate. That was my main reason. Like you said, I know you don't run hot-tempered anymore. I was just looking for a fucking excuse to cut you a break on this time."

Aw, fuck. I was struck mute for a minute, trying to work out what to say. The prospect, Gypsy, saved my ass by not only setting our refilled drinks in front of us, but two shot glasses of tequila as well.

"Shots always make a good reset button."

Huffing out a laugh, I picked up the tequila and held it out for Mac to click his glass against mine. Then we downed them together and while the alcohol was still burning my throat, he pulled me in for a rough, back-slap hug, resetting our friendship before releasing me and slamming his empty shot glass down on the bar.

"You're more than my club brother, Taz. And no matter what comes your way, I will always have your back. You hear me?"

I nodded and grabbed the beer I'd initially ordered from the Prospect, feeling awkward at the emotion swirling around us.

"Yeah, same back at you, mate. Now let's get over

there to see what chaos my sister is planning with my woman."

Mac laughed and slapped me on the back. "You're in so much trouble if those two decide to gang up on you."

Yeah, wasn't that the truth. But I was kinda looking forward to it.

I turned to face the women, barely aware of Mac moving. I had my sister back. My baby sister, whom I'd thought was dead was here in the Charon MC clubhouse, sitting next to my old lady with my daughter, who'd now woken up from her nap, on her lap. Fuck, it was enough to bring a grown man to his knees. It really was.

Flick looked over, and our gazes locked for a moment before she winced and shifted her focus back to my sister. I sighed. Life wasn't all sunshine and rainbows. I had no clue how to process the fact my woman had hidden this shit from me.

Scout came to stand beside me, taking the glass the prospect handed over before speaking to me. "Pretty sure she was trying to protect you too, brother."

I shook my head, then downed the rest of my beer before responding.

"Yeah, well, that shit ain't right. I'm supposed to be the one doing the protecting. I don't need a fucking guard."

Scout gripped my shoulder, giving a squeeze, but before he could say a word, I shrugged out of his hold. "You ain't exactly my favorite person right now either, Prez. You sure you want to be this close to my brand of crazy?"

I was feeling on edge and looking for someone to lash out against.

Fucker rolled his eyes. "Quit the drama, Taz. For the record, I wanted to hand you a rifle and wish you luck hunting when I first heard that bastard was coming our way." He sighed again. "No one believes you're still that hothead you were when you were younger. Hell, none of us are who we were all those years ago. We all change. Your old lady and child were in danger, so I'd be more worried if you didn't go a little crazy. Considering I went halfway across the fucking country to wipe out an entire MC when they came after my woman and son, I'm not gonna judge on that one."

I scoffed and took a drink as I remembered how Scout led the charge to take down the Ice Riders MC after they came and held a few of our women at gunpoint, sending Marie into early labor. Thankfully, both Marie and their son, Joey, were fine now.

"Just tread carefully with her, brother. Don't go throwing away all you have because of this one misstep, especially when you know full well she did it out of love for you."

I couldn't deal with any of this shit right now. I needed to get out of here. To clear my head. Maybe then I could think clearly and work out what the fuck I was going to do about what Flick had done.

"I'm going for a ride. Be back later."

Turning toward the bar, I handed my empty glass to

the prospect before heading for the door. I knew Scout and the other club brothers would keep my family safe, but I couldn't be here anymore. I needed some time with my bike on the open road.

Flick

My heart didn't just break, it shattered into tiny little pieces as Taz stormed out of the clubhouse. Sniffling, I blinked back tears as Mac and Eagle both slipped out after my man. His club brothers would make sure he was safe and stop him if he tried to do anything too reckless, but damn, it fucking hurt he didn't even say goodbye to me or Lolly.

"What'd you do to have him running from you? Sorta figured he'd be glued to your side for a while after today."

Jacie was grinning at Lolly as she played with my daughter, but her tone was serious without any cheer or humor.

"We didn't tell him we knew Gordon was coming."

She cringed. "Oh, yeah. With how protective he is, I'm sure that'll have him raging for a while."

I frowned. "You were only little when you last saw him. How do you know him so well?"

A blush raced over her face. "Ah, well. I may have used my skills to keep tabs on him. You know… just maybe."

I nudged her shoulder with mine. "Don't be embarrassed. In your shoes, I'd have done the same thing." I sighed. "But, yeah, Taz is not happy with any of us. Although, it looked like he and Mac sorted their shit out earlier over at the bar."

"Mamamama!"

Lolly lunged from Jacie's lap at me, forcing me to put all my focus on my little girl to make sure the wriggling toddler didn't end up on the floor. I rubbed my nose against hers.

"Yes, my darling girl? Did I stop giving you all my attention?"

She giggled with a grin, and my heart melted into a pile of goo. I loved my daughter as much as I loved my husband. My stomach churned as I wondered if I hadn't destroyed my family with what I'd done.

Jacie spoke quietly, "Why didn't you tell him?"

I thought that through for a few moments before I answered.

"Well, we didn't know for sure he was in town yet, but mostly I wanted to save him from having to deal with it all. Not sure if you looked into me, but I'm not exactly helpless. Not that I expected to be able to take out Gordon by myself. That's why I'd spoken to Scout and Mac about it. With their help, I'd hoped to get the situation dealt with without Taz ever having to know Gordon had come anywhere near him. Especially this close to the anniversary. He struggles enough this time of year."

Jacie winced. "I always hated that they separated us.

When I was younger, I'd beg my foster father to take me to Taz or bring him back to us." She shook her head before frowning at me. "You had to know it was a pipe dream that Taz wouldn't find out what you were up to."

I nodded as the ache in my chest increased. "Yeah, it was naive of me. I just wanted to save my man some pain. But in the end, I nearly got Lolly and I killed."

I wasn't going to pretend Gordon had anything other than pain planned for me and my daughter, all to cause Taz as much agony as possible. I'd nearly made his life so much worse.

"Thankfully, Don—I mean Taz—is smarter than you guys gave him credit for, and worked it out. Got there to snipe my bastard of a father and save the day. He totally deserves a reward for that, you know?"

I raised an eyebrow at her. "A reward? What, like his long-lost sister moving to town? That would be a great reward."

A familiar snicker filled the air a moment before Silk plopped down beside me, Raven clinging to her until he saw Lolly. Then he was all about wanting to be put down to play with his friend. I lowered Lolly down to stand on the floor as Silk did the same with her boy.

"Sorry I'm late, I had to finish up a tatt before picking up Raven and coming over." She leaned around me. "Hi, I'm Silk. You must be Jacie, Taz's sister, right?"

Jacie's eyes went wide. "Damn. How'd you know who I am already?"

I couldn't help but chuckle, as did Silk. "You'll learn

nothing spreads quite like gossip in an MC."

Silk smirked at Jacie. "My old man is Eagle, Taz's spotter. He was with Taz when he took out the threat earlier. He called me as soon as the danger was over to tell me what had happened."

She wrapped an arm around my shoulders and pulled me in for a short hug. "You doing okay, doll?"

I nodded. "Yeah, I'm fine."

Jacie scoffed. "Physically, anyhow. My big bro ain't a happy camper, if you know what I mean, and she's got a good case of the guilts going on."

I cocked an eyebrow at Jacie. "You done? Or you wanna keep psychoanalyzing me?"

Jacie just grinned and shrugged. "I'm guessing she's a friend, so stop trying to pull the wool over her eyes. Let her help. Taz won't stay away for long, so we don't have time to beat around the bush."

"Wool over my eyes?" Silk shook her head. "Yeah, you're definitely your brother's sister. Trying to confuse us with Aussie slang already."

Jacie winked Silk's way but before she could say anything, her phone rang. She pulled it out and cringed before mumbling under her breath, "Dammit. I'd hoped this call wouldn't come for a couple more days."

With a falsely happy voice, she answered, "Hey, Dad, what's up?"

She winced, then spoke in her normal tone. "Yeah, I'm in Texas. How'd you find out?"

She held the phone away from her ear as she stood and

headed toward the back of the clubhouse. Guess she pulled the same stunt with her foster father that I had with Taz, and we were both in the shit because of it.

Chapter 6

Friday 13th April 2019
Flick

On autopilot, I cut up a few strawberries, half a banana and some apple, put them in a bowl and slid them onto the tray of Lolly's highchair.

"Hmm, yum!"

My daughter's enthusiasm for her breakfast made me smile, bringing a much-needed flash of joy to my sober mood. Leaving her to feed herself, I grabbed the yogurt from the fridge and scooped some into a bowl while blinking back tears. Today was Lolly's first birthday. Taz should be here. As a couple, we should be looking after our baby girl and showering her in love. But instead, it was just her and me.

Moving to sit next to her chair, I started feeding her spoonfuls of the mixed berry flavored yogurt between her mashing fistfuls of fruit into her mouth.

"You sure do make a mess, baby girl."

She gave me a grin, flashing her four perfectly formed little teeth. Two on the top and two on the bottom, front and center. My heart softened and I leaned in to kiss her temple. She would always be the center of my world, and I needed to pull myself together to be happy today to give her a wonderful first birthday, even if Taz didn't turn up.

It'd been nearly two full weeks since everything went down with Gordon, and it had been that long since I'd slept in the same bed as my husband. This was the longest we'd gone without being intimate with each other. Even after Lolly's birth when we couldn't have sex, we'd gotten creative with each other's bodies.

I missed him. And not just for sex, although he was damn good at it. I missed his humor, his smile. He was always so damn cheeky and such a flirt. He would constantly touch me, sliding his palm down my back as he passed me or giving me quick kisses before moving onto whatever he needed to do.

It was as though I was missing a limb without him close. Lolly'd noticed too. She often would look around the room, clearly searching for him. And she could say Dad now. Most days it seemed to be her favorite word, and how could I explain that her normally very affectionate, over-the-top daddy wasn't anywhere near her because Mommy had made him so angry, he couldn't stand the sight of her?

I hiccupped a sob as I turned to toss the empty bowl into the sink. Grabbing a washcloth, I wiped down Lolly.

"How about a bath before we get dressed for your party?"

"Dadadadada."

More tears leaked from my eyes at her sweet babbling. Lifting her from the chair, I cuddled her close.

"Hopefully, he'll be at the party, baby girl. Mama misses him too."

A loud knock on the front door had me heading that way, wondering who it was.

Glancing through the peephole, my breath caught. Fumbling in my rush, I eventually got the door unlocked and thrown open.

"What on earth are you doing here?"

Before I'd finished speaking, I pulled Jacie in for a tight hug. Lolly giggled as she got mashed into the group squeeze. Jacie had to rush back to Australia after her foster father called, and I'd not heard from her since.

Releasing her from the embrace, she turned to grab a couple suitcases that were next to her.

"Ah, Jacie, what's going on?"

She grinned at me and poked her tongue out at Lolly, getting another giggle out of my girl.

"I'm moving in!"

I frowned in confusion. "What?"

She rolled the cases in and shut the door before turning back to me.

"That offer to stay here is still open, right?"

I shook myself free from my shocked stupor. "Of course! Did Taz know you were coming?"

She blushed and slid a palm around the back of her neck.

I groaned. "Jacie! Seriously?"

She winced. "I thought it would be a nice surprise this time. And it's just in time for my niece's birthday. Hey, Lolly, got some love for Auntie Jacie?"

Jacie held her arms out, and Lolly happily went from me to her aunt, who cuddled and cooed over her.

"You need to make sure to tell Taz I didn't know you were coming... not that he's been around long enough for me to have told him." I mumbled the last part as I turned away, but I didn't get far because Jacie grabbed my wrist and pulled me back.

"What do you mean, he's not been around?"

Those damn tears I hated so much were back, tracking down my cheeks no matter how fast I dashed them away.

"He just needs more time."

She growled. "No, he doesn't. He needs a kick in the arse. And I intend to give it to him. Do you know where he is?"

I took a deep breath before I could speak. "I think he's been sleeping at the clubhouse. Not sure what he's been doing with his days."

Or his nights. He'd been such a damn manwhore before we'd gotten together. I prayed he hadn't fallen into old habits these past weeks.

Fire flashed in her blue eyes that were so like her brother's, my heart ached all over again.

She pressed a kiss to Lolly's cheek then handed her back.

"I will go find my dipshit brother and get him sorted."

I cuddled Lolly in close, taking comfort from her

sweet baby scent and the way her little fingers clutched at me.

"Her party starts in two hours at the clubhouse. If you could make sure he gets there at least, I'd be grateful."

Then unable to hold myself together any longer, I turned and headed upstairs. I'd give Lolly a nice long bath before I got her into her pretty party dress.

Jacie

Frustration had me driving faster than I normally did as I raced from my brother's place to the Charon MC clubhouse. It wasn't until I pulled past an open gate and parked beside the three other cars that I started to question my decision to come here. A young guy sauntered over to me from where he'd been leaning against the building when I rolled up.

"Hey, pretty lady, somethin' I can help you with?"

I ran my gaze up and down his lean body. Not bad. I mentally shook my head. I was not here to scope out the sights, no matter how pleasant they might be. Since I didn't remember seeing this bloke the last time I was here, I doubted he'd know who I was. Great. Hopefully I could convince him to let me through.

"I'm looking for my brother, Taz. Flick thought he might be here."

With a frown, he stood straight and pulled his phone out. Naturally, he'd have to ring someone to get permission. I tapped my fingers over the steering wheel while I took in the yard around me. Carefully focusing in on the several bikes that were parked in a neat row, I couldn't see the green Harley I knew Taz normally rode. Did he have more than one bike? Dammit. If he wasn't here, I had no clue where to go looking.

Lost in thought, I jerked when the man came back to my window.

"Keys said he'll meet you inside."

With that, he wandered back to lean against the clubhouse near the door. A lazy panther on guard duty. With a sigh, I rolled my shoulders and got out of my car. With my head high, I marched over to the entrance and headed in. I paused in the dim interior, allowing my eyes a moment to adjust.

"Jacie, didn't know you were back in town. When'd you get in?"

Keys spoke as he came out from a hallway and headed straight to me.

"Just got in. Went to surprise my brother, but he's not where he should be. You know anything about that?"

With a sad smile he shook his head. "He's not here. Not sure where he is. Follow me back to my office and I'll see if I can't track him down. I know he wouldn't knowingly miss his girl's birthday party today."

I followed him away from the main room. "What's happened since I left? Flick looks like shit, and she had no idea where Taz was. He's not stepping out on her, is he?"

If he was, I'd kick his ass for real.

With a heavy sigh, Keys passed through a doorway. He didn't answer me until he was sitting behind a desk covered in monitors with a laptop in the center.

"Your brother loves Flick and Lolly. I can't imagine he'd even look at another woman at this point. He's struggling with wrapping his head around what happened. Didn't help a few of the club also knew about Gordon, and everyone kept it from him. Not sure what he needs to reset, but hopefully he works it out soon."

After tapping at the keyboard for a minute, he sat back and looked to where I was still standing just inside the door.

"You just visiting for your niece's birthday, or you moving?"

Forcing a smile, I raised an eyebrow at him. "Why do you want to know?"

He waved a hand around his desk. "Because we need more people who are already trained to work with Athena Security. Scout wasn't blowing smoke up your ass. We've finally found some office space that'll work, so we can move it out of here. We've got brothers keen to join, but they need training. That all takes time."

Tapping my fingers against my thigh, I stared at Keys and weighed up how much I should tell him.

"Close the door and come sit down, Jacie. Tell me what the fuck happened after your dad summoned you back home. Your secrets are safe with me. Nothin' will leave this room that you don't want to."

It wasn't like I had a ton of options, and my brother trusted this man. Making the decision to take a chance on him and the club, I turned, closed the door and strode over to the chair in front of the desk.

"You already know I broke rules to keep an eye on Gordon. I used resources without permission. Dad did what he could, but it went over his head." I shrugged. "I didn't want him to lose his job by trying to keep me mine, so I quit before we both could get fired. I brought everything important to me with me. I did plan to move here, but I know there's paperwork and shit that'll need to be done to make it all legal, and I might have to go back to Australia until it all processes."

Keys tapped at the keyboard again before turning back to me. "You want to work for the club with Athena Security?"

I smiled at him, "Well, it's that or I go apply down at the local supermarket for a checkout job. Although, not sure that'll get me a work visa."

He laughed. "You're gonna fit in here just fine, girl. Come around this side of the desk, and I'll show you where your dumbass brother currently is."

I moved to stand beside him and took in the various screens, most filled with camera feeds. "Damn, Keys. Do you have the whole bloody town wired?"

He smirked. "Something like that. The ones on the main roads in and out of town, I try to monitor, but most of what I've set up only gets used if needed. I'm not into invading people's privacy. I need to know those I care for are safe."

I nodded, a little in awe at how big a set-up he had, then my gaze caught on the screen that held Taz. With ear protection on, he stood with his legs braced as he held a handgun in front of him and with how it kicked in his grip, I knew he was emptying the clip quickly. His face was drawn, and he had the start of a beard going. He looked as bad as Flick.

"Is the shooting range here in town?"

He raised an eyebrow at me. "I thought you've been keeping an eye on your brother?"

I scoffed. "Not on a stalker level."

"Flick's uncle owns the local gun range and shop. He had a heart attack not long ago. Taz and Flick have stepped in to help him run a lot of it." He nodded at the screen. "Guessing he's venting his frustrations on paper targets down there."

With hands on hips, I glared at the image of my big brother.

"Since he doesn't look like he's packing up any time soon, guess I'll go give him a boot in the arse so he'll make it to his daughter's birthday party today."

I was about to turn when Keys pulled up another window, this time with what looked like a real estate listing.

"Before you go, what do you think?"

Leaning forward, I took the mouse and scrolled through the photos and read the listing.

"Looks good. I mean, I don't know Bridgewater well

enough to give comment on the location, but the size and number of rooms looks good. Especially if you can get someone to rent that apartment over the top for extra income."

When he stayed silent, I stood and after folding my arms over my chest, stared him in the eyes.

"Stop beating around the bush, Keys. Speak plainly."

"I know Taz and Flick offered you a room in their place, but not sure you wanna be listening in on them on a nightly basis, yeah? Would you consider being our in-house emergency on-call person? Of course, you'd need to do a trial period first and prove yourself, during which time you'd live up there like any renter would."

Excitement bubbled in me. No way would Athena have all the red tape that had driven me nuts at the AFP. And, assuming my brother pulled his head out of his arse, I'd be working closer with him and Flick.

"It's definitely something I'd consider. Let me think on it while I go sort out Taz, and I'll let you know by the end of the day."

Keys gave me a nod and smile. "Looking forward to your answer. Write your number down and I'll text you directions so you can go kick his ass for us."

With hope sparking within me at the new start I could make for myself here in Bridgewater, I headed back out of the clubhouse with a spring in my step.

Taz

Every round I fired from the brand new 9mm Glock tactical eased my soul a little more. But it wasn't enough. Nothing in the past twelve days had been able to shake this bone-deep weariness I had going on. It was getting worse each day.

I was pretty sure I knew what would cure it, but I wasn't ready to face Flick yet. Her betrayal was still too fresh.

When I ran out of bullets, I popped out the magazine and reached for the box of ammo to refill it when someone smacked my shoulder. Hard. Putting the weapon down on the bench, I pulled out my earplugs as I turned with a scowl, ready to tear a strip of whoever had interrupted my range time.

But when I saw who stood there, hands on hips looking furious, I grinned.

"Jacie!"

Reaching forward, I pulled my baby sister in against me. She tried to stay stiff, pulling away, but it was only seconds before she softened and returned my embrace.

"Hey, big bro. You're a hard man to track down."

I released her and she stepped away, her frown returning.

"I find it relaxing to shoot shit." I shrugged.

She crossed her arms and raised an eyebrow at me. "Even on your daughter's first birthday?"

I closed my eyes as my whole body slumped. Fuck. "I haven't been watching the date."

"My first stop was your house. Wanna know how your wife or daughter are doing?"

A flash of rage had me snapping at Jacie before I thought it through. "Did Flick know you were coming?" Was this something else she'd kept from me?

With wide eyes, she held a palm up. "Whoa. Stop right fucking there. No one knew I was coming today. It was a last-minute thing I managed to pull together, so figured I'd surprise you all for my favorite niece's birthday. I thought Flick was overreacting when she'd asked I make sure you knew she didn't keep it from you. Are you seriously still holding that against her?"

I settled a bit that my old lady hadn't further betrayed me, but I was not having my little sister lecture me.

Folding my arms over my chest, I glared into Jacie's gaze. "She kept information from me that nearly cost me another family!"

Her jaw clenched as she ground her teeth for a few moments before she spoke. "I'm wondering why you give a fuck, Donny? Seems to me, you're the one who's thrown them away. If you're really so fucking hurt that you nearly lost your wife and daughter, why are you here shooting paper cutouts and not with them? Not making sure they know they're the most important thing in your world." She shook her head. "Flick had no idea where you were today. I don't think she's known where you've been for the last two weeks. How'd you think that makes her feel, considering how *you* felt when you didn't know where they were for just a few hours?"

She paused to release a long breath on a sigh. "You need to get your head on straight, big brother. I get me coming back from the dead threw you for a loop. I get you're probably still mad at me for it, even though I was a fucking child and had no say in what happened back then. You married an FBI agent. A trained woman. And she wasn't planning on rushing in to save the day on her own. She called in your club to back her up. She was trying to fucking save you from some extra pain. That's it. Your woman loved you enough to try to save you some pain. Yeah, it backfired. But you were there when it counted, and you saved them. Tell me, Donny—why save them if you were just gonna throw them both away afterward?"

Spinning on her heel, she strode toward the exit but stopped with her hand on the door. "Regardless of how you now feel about your wife, your daughter is only a year old and didn't do a damn thing wrong, yet she's lost her daddy and has no fucking clue why. You have an hour to get yourself to the clubhouse for her party. Maybe I'll see you there."

And with that, she was gone, and I was alone in the range with nothing but my thoughts.

Fuck. Jacie was right about Lolly. She'd done nothing wrong, had been through a really scary experience, and now I'd vanished on her. What had Flick told our baby girl? I looked at my watch, noting the time. Right. An hour. I scrubbed a hand over my jaw and the short beard that had grown in over the last two weeks. First, I had to get everything packed up and cleaned away here, then hopefully I'd have time for a shower and a shave, and I had to get my fucking head on straight. I also needed to fucking grow a set and sit down to talk things out with my woman.

I needed her in my life. Her and Lolly both.

I also had to corner my sister for another chat. How long was she here for, this time? She'd had to rush off after her foster father called her the evening after we took down Gordon and I hadn't heard from her since, so I had no fucking clue what her plans were.

Chapter 7

Flick

Within the first ten minutes of arriving at the clubhouse, Lolly's pretty purple dress with big pink flowers on it was now also sporting a smear of dirt right down the front. Not that I minded. I'd rather expected it, actually. Raven, Cleo and she were well acquainted with the clubhouse yard and were doing what they normally did— running around the large area having a great time. Ariel and Ashlynn, who were both six, had started off with them, but had now gone off on their own, no doubt planning some sort of chaos. The club didn't call them double trouble without good reason. Sparrow was also with the younger trio, Cleo not letting her adopted big sister to get far from her. It was sweet to see the teen being so happy to do her baby sister's bidding. Cleo was like that, though. The girl managed to get everyone near her wrapped around her little finger in no time at all.

The club had rescued Sparrow from a cartel brothel in L.A. about six months ago, and she'd refused to stay with the other kids and women to wait for the authorities.

Instead, she'd stowed away in the club's van. When they'd discovered her, she begged to come home with them and in the end, Mac and Zara had adopted her. In just the last few months the teen had blossomed. She was getting regular counseling and tutoring, and it looked like by the fall she'd be ready to enroll in the local school where she'd make some friends and be a normal teenager. We were all so happy for her.

Sparrow's attention wasn't one hundred percent on her sister, though. Nope. Every few minutes her gaze would linger on a certain man standing in a group of younger brothers and prospects hanging out to the side of the yard, away from the families. They'd all helped set up and some of the prospects needed to hang around for their turns on either guard or bar duty. It wouldn't be long until the ones not needing to work cleared out. Kid parties didn't really spell fun for men in their late teens to early twenties. They'd no doubt be back later tonight, well after Lolly's party was done and dusted.

I glanced around, looking for Mac. Most of the club knew there was something happening between Jazz and Sparrow, but as far as I knew, neither had done anything about the attraction, mainly because Mac would skin Jazz alive if he dared touch the teen. I chuckled at the glare Mac was sending the young man's way.

Zara came up beside me. "Sparrow's gonna die a virgin."

Silk scoffed. "Nah, she'll be fine. She'll just need to learn to be real creative, is all."

That had us all laughing. As the niece of the club's previous VP, Silk had firsthand knowledge of how hard it was to get laid when you had the Charon MC's officers protecting you.

The sound of a Harley pulling up had me growing serious and turning toward the door, praying it'd be Taz who walked out next. When it opened and Arrow came through, Tabitha trailing behind him holding a present, my heart dropped.

Zara wrapped an arm around my shoulders, pulling me in against her. "He'll be here."

I nodded but had serious doubts as I began to wonder if he even remembered it was Lolly's birthday. Tears pricked my eyes, but I blinked them away.

"Is it too early to start drinking?"

Silk gave me a sad smile before she shrugged. "It's five o'clock somewhere, yeah? I'll be right back."

She slipped her phone out as she headed inside, and I knew she'd be either messaging Taz directly, or her man, Eagle, about finding Lolly's missing daddy. Zara gave me another squeeze before she let her hand drop away.

"Mammmma!"

I dropped down to my knees as my sweet girl came barreling my way, hands reaching for me. I spread my arms and let her run into me, nearly knocking me over with her crash-hug.

"Hello, baby girl. You having fun?"

She snuggled in for a few moments before she pulled away to look up at me. The seriousness in her gaze reminded me so much of Taz, tears threatened again. Before I cracked wide open and started bawling because my daughter was looking into my soul, the rear door smacking shut broke the moment.

Lolly looked to the sound and her little face lit up. Thinking it must be Taz to get that reaction, I brushed the dirt off her dress and my shirt before I released her. She was off like a rocket before I could stand and turn.

My heart both warmed and sank as Jacie crouched down to clutch Lolly to her.

"Hey, it's my favorite niece! Happy birthday, Lolly."

Jacie handed her a toy koala that Lolly cuddled in against her as she rested her little head on her aunt's shoulder. I sighed as they walked over to me.

"Hey, Flick, you doing okay?"

I shrugged, trying to not fucking cry. Jacie had the same eyes as her brother, and it was nearly more than I could take. When I stayed silent, Jacie winced then she lowered down to set Lolly on her feet. "Why don't you go play for a bit, Lolly?" Before she finished speaking, my daughter was off, heading to Cleo and Raven to show off her new toy.

Before Jacie could say another word, Silk reappeared with shot glasses and a bottle of whiskey that she settled down on the table behind us. She'd barely filled the first glass when I snatched it up and downed it.

"Damn, girl. My brother's a bloody moron."

Silk nodded Jacie's way and refilled my glass. A shudder ran through me after I downed the second. It was eleven in the morning, way earlier than I'd normally drink, but I didn't care. Not today. There were plenty of adults here to help me take care of Lolly, and I needed to get out of my head for a little while. I had my third shot pressed to my lips when the rear door opened once more, and this time I didn't bother to look over. Accepting Taz wasn't coming, I downed my shot and tried not to think about how I'd lost my man for good when all I'd wanted to do was save him some pain.

Taz

A couple customers coming in had held up my getting out of the shop. Originally, I was just going to close for the rest of the day, but it seemed everyone wanted to restock their ammo before the weekend. I'd called in Gus, who'd been more than happy to take over. Instead of joining today's party, Flick's uncle was going to come around to our place for lunch tomorrow to celebrate Lolly's birthday. He was a lot better about being around the club since we'd saved Flick, but he still didn't want to be inside the clubhouse. I'd vowed we'd get him in there one day, but that day wouldn't be today.

"Why you working at all today, boy?"

I winced at his question as he walked through the door.

"I haven't been watching the date. Didn't realize it was the thirteenth."

That earned me a hard stare. "Do we need to have words, boy?"

I shook my head. "No, sir. No words needed. My sister already gave me the lecture, and if I can ever get out of here, I'll be on my way to try to fix things."

"Well, getcha ass moving. I can handle this place with my eyes closed. Go fix shit with my niece."

I didn't need to be told twice. It was only seconds before I was grabbing my keys and dashing out the door. I'd been a damn fool. That's what I'd come to realize since Jacie had ripped me a new one. If Flick and my roles had been reversed, I'd have done the same fucking thing. I hadn't married a woman who needed to be protected like some hot house flower, I'd married a warrior. A partner. My equal.

And I fucking missed her like crazy. Her and Lolly both.

It was a bitter pill to swallow that by being so fucking butt-hurt over Flick's keeping shit from me nearly costing me my family, I'd potentially cost myself exactly that. Such a moron.

Swinging my leg over the seat, I wasted no time in getting my ride started and headed straight for the clubhouse, hoping like hell my woman hadn't given up on me yet. Ignoring speed limits, I made it in record time. Moments after pulling in, I was off and striding to the door. The prospect manning the door shook his head at me with a frown, making it clear the whole damn club no doubt knew how badly I'd fucked up, but I ignored him.

One of the first things I learned after joining the Charons was how quickly gossip spread around this place.

Jogging through the empty clubhouse, I slipped out the rear door and bit back a curse as I watched Flick down a shot of whiskey. Before I could go over to her, I had a squealing toddler wrapped around my legs.

"Daddy! Daaaaaddy! Daddy!"

I swung Lolly up in my arms and blew a raspberry into her neck, getting me a giggle as my beard tickled her soft skin. Shifting her to sit on my hip, I took in the stuffed koala she shoved under my nose proudly.

"Oh, that's a very nice koala, baby girl. Did your Aunty Jacie give that to you?"

She garbled in baby speak for a bit then wriggled to be let down. As soon as her little feet hit the ground, she was off. I watched her, Raven and Cleo playing for a few moments before I braved turning back toward my old lady.

Jacie, Silk and Zara surrounded her, all frowning as Flick argued with Silk, who held a bottle of whiskey out of my woman's reach. Clearly, the other women were trying to cut Flick off and she wasn't having it. I rubbed the ache in my chest as a pang of guilt hit me hard that I'd driven her to this. She wasn't one to drink much, especially this early in the day. And definitely not when our daughter was near and might need her.

While Lolly was too little to remember anything about today once she was older, Flick would. And she'd never forgive herself for spending Lolly's first birthday drunk.

Rolling my shoulders while blowing out a breath, I headed over to her and wrapping one hand around her wrist, took the empty glass from her and handed it off to Silk. With a snarl, she tried to tug her arm free but quickly gave up when I wouldn't release her. Instead, she aimed a glare my way.

"Let me go and give me my damn glass back! I'm not done."

"You're more than done, hellcat." I didn't take my gaze off her as I spoke to the others.

"Ladies, please keep an eye on Lolly for us while I take Flick inside for a coffee."

"You've got twenty minutes before we come looking for her." The anger in Zara's voice was barely leashed. Guess I was in the doghouse with everyone today.

I nodded then scooped my woman up in my arms.

"Put me down." She wriggled as she growled out the words, but I wasn't letting her go.

"Stop making a scene, hellcat."

With a sharp inhale that I took for the curse it was, she wrapped a fist in my cut but otherwise stilled as she noticed we had the attention of all the adults in the yard. She held herself stiff against me as I strode toward the clubhouse, but it didn't matter. I'd missed her like crazy and having her in my arms was already soothing the ache I'd had in my soul these past days. It also had my cock rock-hard and ready for action, throbbing to get inside my woman. Although, I doubted I was going to get any relief in that department any time soon. Blue balls were most likely in my immediate future, but I'd deal. If it took a little while to seduce my wife, I could handle it.

I didn't stop until we were alone in the kitchen. I lowered her down onto a stool before I moved over to the row of pod machines and set one going.

"Lolly's missed you."

Her quiet words were like a knife to my gut, and I ground my teeth as I waited on her coffee to brew. Once it was done, I tossed the used pod in the trash then returned to where Flick sat, watching me with tears in her eyes. My tough woman rarely cried. I hated I'd brought her to her knees like this. Part of me wanted to know if she'd missed me too, but asking would only make her more upset so I didn't go there.

Setting the mug on the table in front of her, I nodded at it. "Start drinking, kitty. Need to get you sober for our girl's party. Then tonight we'll talk and get everything sorted."

Her body slumped, her shoulders curling forward as she hunched over, wrapping her palms around the hot drink. I didn't miss the tear slipping down her cheek and it was another gut punch.

Chapter 8

Flick

For the rest of the day, I was on edge. Lolly really had missed her daddy and didn't ever let him get far away from her. He was acting like his old self, lots of smiles and jokes, but there was an edge to it.

I'd managed to slip inside a few times to go to the bar to sneak in another shot or two. Not enough that I was drunk, but just enough to have me mostly able to focus on something other than Taz's words to me earlier. What had he meant by "get everything sorted"? Was he done with me? Or did he want to come back home and work things out?

With the party now over, I sighed as I loaded another box of presents into the trunk of my SUV. The entire club had spoiled my girl rotten, and she had more toys than she could possibly play with before she grew out of them. Maybe I could let Lolly pick out favorites then donate the rest to charity.

My thoughts were jumping around so much I was struggling to stay focused. Shutting the trunk, I stepped back but stiffened when a hand rested on my shoulder.

"Don't you dare throw me, Flick."

Taz's growled words had my lips twitching despite my low mood. Memories of that first night in Styx when he'd crept up behind me. Surprised when he grabbed my shoulder, instinct had taken over and before I knew what I'd done, I had him on his back on the floor. Some of the brothers still gave him grief over it.

"Well, stop sneaking up on me!"

Fuck, but it felt good to banter like we always had. He turned me in his arms and within moments, I found myself pressed between the back door of the SUV and his warm body. Looking up into his face, I got lost in his baby blues.

"Fuck, but I've missed you, kitten."

His gravelly tone had shivers running down my spine. Before I could respond, he lowered his mouth, pressing his soft lips to mine. Moaning, I wrapped my arms around his neck to make sure he wasn't going anywhere anytime soon. He buried a hand in my hair and tugged until I opened my mouth on a gasp, then his tongue swept in and like I always had, I melted for my man. My other half.

Taz had always been so possessive and alpha male when it came to anything intimate. Kissing, sex, fooling around… if he was near me, he was an absolute caveman about getting my attention. Except if Lolly needed me, then he'd be a total pushover for whatever our baby girl wanted. Our daughter had her daddy firmly wrapped around her little finger.

Speaking of Lolly, Taz was supposed to be watching her. Forcing my brain to kick back into gear, I pushed against his chest until with a growl, he broke the kiss.

"Where's Lolly?"

His eyes were bright with his arousal, not that his massive erection pressing against me left me with any doubt over how horny my man was, and it took him a few moments to respond.

"Jacie kidnapped her. Said something about overdue aunt bonding time or something."

I lifted a hand to cup his bearded jaw. It looked like he hadn't faired any better than me during our separation.

"Let's go get her and head home, Taz. We have to talk before we get hot and heavy, and we don't need an audience for it."

With a shuddering breath, he closed his eyes before he pressed a kiss to my forehead, which had another shiver running down my spine. Stepping away, he took my hand and led me back inside the clubhouse. Once through the door, I spotted Jacie, Sparrow, Cleo and Lolly over in the corner. Silk had taken Raven home already, so it was an all-female party now. Before we got more than a few steps, Zara stepped into our path, forcing Taz to stop or trample her.

With how Taz had tensed up, I spoke before he could. "What's up, Zara?"

Her gaze switched from me to Taz before returning to me. "I was just thinking it might be a good idea for Jacie and Lolly to have a sleepover at our place. You can come over in the morning and have breakfast with us all."

Pulling my hand free from Taz's grip, I threw myself at my friend, giving her a tight hug.

"Thank you! We will definitely take you up on that offer." Releasing Zara, I looked over to where the girls were all playing as I mentally worked out the logistics. "I'll leave my car here for Jacie to take Lolly back in, and I'll go with Taz."

Taz wrapped an arm around my middle and pulled me back against him. "You on the back of my bike sounds like a fantastic fucking idea, kitten. But if we go say goodbye to Lolly, all hell will break loose, and we'll never get away without her."

I winced but nodded. He was right. Lolly had seriously missed her daddy these past twelve days and would not be impressed with him wanting to leave her again.

Zara chuckled. "Give me your keys then head out. I'll explain to Jacie what's going on. Between Jacie and Sparrow, we'll keep Lolly busy enough she won't notice you both have snuck away."

I wasn't so sure about that, but the temptation of being snuggled up behind Taz on his bike for a nice, long ride was too good to resist.

Pulling my keys out, I dropped them into Zara's outstretched palm. "Let us know if she gets upset and you need us to come get her, or if she won't go down to sleep."

I'd barely finished speaking when Taz grabbed my hand and towed me toward the front door. Chuckling as I nearly had to jog to keep up with my man, my heart already felt lighter.

Someone was keen to get me alone.

It gave me hope that we were going to get through this, although I wasn't looking forward to the talking part of the evening. We'd both fucked up, but I'd been the one to create the rift to begin with.

Taz

When Flick had asked to take the long way home, I happily obliged her. I never turned down a chance to ride with her wrapped around me on my bike. And I wasn't looking forward to the "we have to talk" part of our night. Couldn't we just fuck it out? Much simpler.

With a sigh, I pulled into our driveway and waited for Flick to dismount before I did the same and followed her inside. Flick kept going till she was in the kitchen.

"You want a beer or something stronger?"

I shook my head. "We both need clear heads, kitten. Water is fine."

She probably didn't realize I noticed how many times she'd slipped into the clubhouse during the day. I was going to be keeping a close eye on my woman for the next couple months to make sure she hadn't developed a drinking problem. Not that it wasn't totally understandable that she'd reached for the crutch of alcohol to cope with the last couple weeks. Hell, everyone knew I'd used it for years before meeting Flick. Sex, booze and tattoos had been my coping mechanisms. Not anymore. Well, I'd sex up my old lady any chance I got, and I'd drink a few beers or whiskeys with the brothers. Hadn't gotten any new ink in a while, though.

Flick handing me a cold glass pulled me from my introspection. Keeping my gaze on her, I made fast work of downing the water before I took her glass and set them both on the sink.

"I know we gotta talk, babe. But I've fucking missed you. Can we talk in bed with me holding you?"

She barked out a laugh, shaking her head as she saw through my ploy easily. "No, we can't *fuck this out*, Taz." She rubbed a palm over the back of her neck. "We need to talk. *Really* talk. Get everything out in the open. Then you can shave off that beard and we'll go to bed."

That made me smirk her way as I stroked the short whiskers that'd grown in. "What? You don't like my new look?"

She shrugged a shoulder. "If you really want to keep it, you can. I'll get used to it, I suppose."

Before she could guess what I was going to do, I grabbed her around the waist and pulled her in against me. Then I lowered my face so I could rub the offending hair over her neck until she was giggling and pushing me away.

"That's why it needs to go! Way too ticklish! Taz,

stop!"

After giving her ear a nip, I pulled back and stared into her eyes, both of us growing serious.

"I'm sorry I stayed away, Flick." Pausing, I struggled to put how I was feeling into words. "I didn't know how to process everything, so I hid away like a fucking coward, and I'm so damn sorry."

She shook her head, tears welling in her eyes. "If I hadn't kept what I knew about Gordon from you, you wouldn't have needed to process anything." She paused to sniff, blinking back her tears. "I honestly was just trying to protect you but ended up nearly destroying everything."

She started sobbing, and I brought her in against me, wrapping my arms around her shaking body as my heart shattered. When she slipped her hands under my cut, snuggling in against me, I buried my face into her hair, ignoring my own tears that leaked down my cheeks as we continued to hold onto each other.

Every one of her sobs was a fresh slice to my soul, but I stayed strong against the storm that was trying to swallow us whole. Rubbing my palms over her back and pressing kisses to her head, I struggled to keep my own emotions bottled up. Eventually, her sobs lessened and after rubbing her face in against my shirt with a shuddering breath, she pulled back and looked up at me with red-rimmed eyes.

"I love you, Felicity. All of you. The hellcat that'll do anything needed to protect those she loves, the curious kitten who wants to explore everything life can gift, and the mama bear that loves deeply and with everything you have. I'm sorry I tried to box up the hellcat part of you. I let fear control me, and in the end, it was me that nearly cost me my family. Forgive me?"

She shook her head as more tears flowed, but before I could panic, she cupped my cheeks in her palms and guided me toward her. I went willingly, and sparks flew over my skin the moment our lips touched. The kiss was slow and deep, a reconnection of souls that I needed more than I needed to breathe.

When she pulled back, I opened my eyes to stare into her gaze, taking in how fucking beautiful my woman was.

"Of course, I forgive you. I love you with all my heart and soul, Donovan. That includes the alpha male warrior side of you, and I guess I tried to box that part of you away too. I should have come to you the second I got off the phone with Greg. If there's ever a next time, I promise that's what I'll do. I'll never risk us like this ever again. Can you move past what I've done? Forgive me?"

Warmth filled my heart. "Yes. We move forward, Flick. Never back." Pausing to press a kiss to her forehead, I smirked at her. "Can we take this to the bedroom now?"

Her laugh was a little watery, but she was wearing a big grin.

"Sure, Taz. Take me to bed and give me everything I've been missing."

"Now, that's something I'm sure I can deliver on. Especially after my two-week dry spell. I have energy to burn, baby!"

Scooping her up in my arms, she laughed and wrapped her arms around my neck as I rushed toward the stairs. Neither of us would be getting much sleep tonight. I had a new mission, and this one was going to be my pleasure to complete.

The End

Other Charon MC Books:

Book 1:
Inking Eagle

Eagle & Silk

Book 2:
Fighting Mac

Mac & Zara

Book 3:
Chasing Taz

Taz & Zara

Book 4:

Claiming Tiny

Tiny & Mercedes (Missy)

Book 5:

Saving Scout

Scout & Marie

Book 6:

Tripping Nitro

Nitro & Cindy

Book 7:

Scout's Legacy

Scout & Marie

Book 8:
Mac's Destiny

Mac & Zara

Book 9:
Losing Bash

Bash

Book 10:
Finding Needles

Needles & Bess

Book 11:
Forging Blade

Blade & Veronica

Book 12:
Taming Keys

Keys & Donna

Book 13:
Breaking Arrow

Arrow & Tabitha

Book 14:
Taz's Guards

Taz & Flick

Book 15:
Shielding Bank

Bank & Bomber

CPSIA information can be obtained
at www.ICGtesting.com
Printed in the USA
BVHW012245150223
658633BV00017B/254

9 781922 942036